IN THE MIDST

A Novel

ADEWUNMI ANIFOWOSHE

Your Store House will always be full of Harvest!!!

The Lord your God is in your midst, a mighty one who will save; he will rejoice over you with gladness; he will quiet you by his love; he will exult over you with loud singing.
Zephaniah 3:17 ESV

DEDICATION

I dedicate this book to my mother who was a rare gem.

A true lover of God who served Him till her death.

Also to my loving Dad who took up mum's place alongside his and has done a great job of it!

Thank you both for the love, care and encouragement always. Forever loved and cherished.

ACKNOWLEDGMENT

This is my first book and I cannot but thank God who instructed me to write this book and typed it through my hands.

I would like to appreciate everyone that walked this journey with me, especially my siblings Muyiwa, Toyin, Ademola and my entire family . And my adopted little sister Georgina.

To the ones who contributed to the success of this book, Tana, Deji, Ashiedu. Thank you for every time you came through with your skill, understanding, and prayer.

To my special Pastor Taiwo, who continually sow the seed of God's words in me; Thank you for believing in me and supporting me to be the best. Pastor Mobs, I feel your prayers. To my dear Pastor Tunde who is always pushing me higher and encouraging me to be the best, God has created me to be.

To the women that step into my mum's shoes, always praying and looking out for me. I really appreciate your constant prayer and love for me, Mummy Melissa Stevens, and Mummy Cecilia Balogun

DISCLAIMER

This is a work of fiction. The names, characters, business, events, and incidents are the products of the author's imagination and are not to be construed as real. Any resemblance to actual persons, living or dead is purely coincidental.

In

The

Midst

Chapter One

Orchard Street was looking beautiful with the trees on both sides almost touching each other. They all looked green and luscious. As they drove down the road, Hannah admired the beautiful street with beautiful houses.

A few residents were looking out their windows in amazement at the many classic cars driving down their neighbourhood. The church was at the bottom of the street, all decorated in white flowers and some sashes. All this decoration just for Auntie Tina and Uncle Stephen's wedding? Hannah beamed with delight, happy to be part of the wedding party.

Everybody was elegantly dressed, and so

was she. "My elegant flowery dress was a perfect fit for my little bridesmaid role"

As they got down from the car, people were seen going into the church. Some were walking alone, while some as a couple. The choir was singing solemnly. It was a beautiful song.

Hannah's mummy went to her side for the last time, to explain her duties for the day to her as she had been doing since the previous night. She was told to walk in front of Auntie Tina, the bride, and beside David, the page boy.

Her mummy looked at her and asked,

"Are you okay?" Hannah's mum asked.

"Mummy, I want to get married too."

"You will, when the time comes. It is

Auntie Tina's day, so let's celebrate with her," replied her mum.

"Ok mummy. But will David be my husband since he's standing next to me the way Uncle Stephen is standing next to Auntie Tina?"

Her mummy laughed.

"You and David are just helping to make Auntie Tina's day beautiful. It doesn't mean you will get married to each other."

Hannah looked sad. She thought it would take too long before she could walk down the aisle.

Her mind wandered. I will love a big white dress with a long tail, and a crown Tiara adorned with diamonds. I will be a tall, slim, and pretty bride while my husband will be tall and handsome.

He will look at me with loving eyes in the presence of our families.

The voice of the vicar jolted her back to reality.

The ceremony went very well, with so much food and drinks for everybody to eat and drink. The adults were dancing and shouting. Everyone was so happy.

Hannah must have sat on one of the decorated seats to rest her already exhausted self when she fell asleep. She saw herself dressed in a lovely sequin flowing wedding gown wearing a diamante crown.

Both were a gorgeous combination, and they looked so beautiful. She also had a lovely pearl necklace on her neck, which was given to her by her mum. It was a perfect wedding setting.

As she looked up to see who her groom was, she felt a hand tap her. She woke up and realised it was a dream.

Standing above her was her sister.

"Hannah, mummy has been calling you since," she said.

"Oh, I'm sorry, I didn't know when I fell asleep," Hannah replied

"You must be exhausted. How did you sleep with all the loud music going on?"

"Hey, Sarah," Hannah excitedly interrupted her.

"I had a lovely dream. I was getting married and…"

Sarah shut her up immediately, "Oh Hannah! Not one of your wedding dreams again, please. Mummy and daddy are in the car waiting for us. It is time to go home."

Hannah wasn't too happy Sarah didn't let her finish telling her about her dream. I guess she's tired of me talking and dressing my dolls in wedding gowns.

Chapter Two

Years later, she's back in the same church as a chief bridesmaid for her elder sister. It was a flood of memories. She remembered the first day she entered this church as a little girl and all she wanted was to get married.

She smiled as she thought to herself, the dreams of a little girl. And though a couple of years have passed, the dream of getting married has not stopped. A few of her friends were now married and as the years went by, she feared her dream was only going to remain just that–a dream.

Today, her elder sister will get married to her soul mate. Sarah and John were college sweethearts.

They met in their first year in college, and since then, they had been inseparable.

John was a nice and kind young man who treated Sarah like an angel. Sarah was the chatterbox, while John was rarely a talker. He even knew how to make her soft-pedal when she was on a talking spree. They complimented each other so well.

Hannah was of great help to Sarah throughout the wedding preparations. She was by Sarah's side and supported in every way she could. She somehow continued to nurse the thoughts that it would be her turn soon, though she was not even in a relationship yet. Her friends and sister had introduced her to a couple of guys in the past, but none had been successful. She knew she was pretty and eloquent; so the problem was not from her. At least, so she thought!

She was also a believer in God's word. *Psalm 139:14, KJV*, *"I will praise thee; for I am fearfully and wonderfully made: marvellous are thy works; and that my soul knoweth right well."* If God says it, then she believes it. She also knows that God makes everything beautiful in His own time.

Her sister's wedding being celebrated today was a clear testimony to that. It appeared she would not get married eventually as the courtship period was taking so long but the day has come and she was getting married. The ceremony went well. Hannah's feet were aching from so much dancing. She noticed a few admirers swooning over her. One of them particularly caught her attention.
He looked more decent in appearance than the rest, so she felt more comfortable letting

him have her contact.

His name was Jonathan, Stephen's friend, who Sarah had tried to introduce to her before now.

She had lost count of all the men she had met, and she was tired of the several introductions too.

She was by the dessert table when she heard his voice.

"Sweet tooth like me?"

She jumped as she thought she was alone by the stand.

"Oh, sorry. I didn't mean to startle you."

"That's okay. It's my cheat day."

"Oh, Diet freak!"

Hannah smiled. "Not really. I am just trying to watch my weight. I promised myself to have my fill of sweet things today, though.

Dieting can continue tomorrow!"

"My name is Jonathan," he said, stretching his hand towards her. Hannah's eyes shot wide while trying to maintain composure. "I am Hannah." "Sarah's sister?" Jonathan asked.

"Yes," Hannah replied.

It was then it occurred to her that this was Jonathan Sarah had been talking about. He was tall, handsome, and soft-spoken.

Chapter Three

The traffic on her way to work was hectic. She was running late as she left home a bit later than the normal time. She was meant to have a meeting with a client this morning. It was a case of a landlord suing his tenant.

He wants her out without giving enough notice. Hannah was hoping the landlord would see reason and settle out of court; as the woman is a struggling single mother with two children.

The lady's husband had died a few months ago and before his death, she did not have any source of income.

This made it particularly difficult to keep up with the rent, coupled with the responsibility of taking care of the children.

The landlord had accepted to see Hannah and the lady today to discuss how to sort the issue.

Hannah checked her time as she muttered a short prayer, "God please let this traffic move." Just before she finished, the traffic eased off. She looked up with a smile. "Thank you, God. I know you always answer me."

Her phone rang. She picked through the car speaker.

"Good morning, Hannah. How are you?" the voice on the other end said. "I'm fine, just in traffic on my way to work." Hannah and Jonathan have been communicating regularly since they met at her sister's wedding.

Hannah was starting to like him, and their conversation was never boring. He always ensured he called her in the morning.

"I hope you will not be late to work," Jonathan added.

"I hope so too because I have an early meeting this morning," replied Hannah.

As they talked, she noticed the traffic situation had improved. "God has answered my prayer; the traffic is going fast now," she gushed to Jonathan.

Jonathan laughed, wrapping up the conversation. "Good for you. I will see you later tonight."

She said her goodbye, and Jonathan dropped the call.

As the call dropped, Hannah wondered why Jonathan never talked about God or acknowledged it whenever she mentioned anything about God. She had tried a few times to ask him about his stand with Christ but she noticed he always avoided the talk. Just like he did now when she mentioned "God had answered her prayer regarding the traffic".

I don't want to end up with a guy that is not born again. The bible says, Do not be yoked together with unbelievers. For what do righteousness and wickedness have in common? Or what fellowship can light have with darkness? I can't have served God this far to end up marrying one that doesn't know God. She decided to have this talk with him. She needed to know if they were on the same page before taking it any further.

She remembered their first date. He had taken her to a fancy restaurant, and when she asked him to pray for their food, he quickly declined and asked her to do the honours. She thought nothing of it, so she dismissed it.

She also remembered one Saturday she invited him to her church for a special program the next day. He declined the invitation, saying he had an appointment to attend to.

After their conversation this morning, memories of the different times when he had refused to pray, refused to come to church with her, or outrightly refused to talk about his faith came flooding through her mind.

She let out a prayer, "God, why do I have to be involved with someone that does not believe in You, after I have waited this long?" As she said the prayer, she felt the

Holy Spirit speaking to her in Jeremiah 5:14: "The Lord God All-Powerful said these things: The people said I would not punish them. So, Jeremiah, the words I give you will be like fire and these people will be like wood.

That fire will burn them up completely." The bible verse startled her, and she felt uneasy. Why will the Holy Spirit remind me of this verse? One thing she knew, however, was that God's word is not in vain and He knows what He's saying.

Chapter Four

Finally, she got to work just a few minutes before the meeting. As she walked into the office, her secretary greeted,

"Good morning, ma'am. Your 11 am appointment is waiting for you in the meeting room."

"Good morning," Hannah replied. "Can you please tell them to give me few minutes to settle down?" Hannah instructed.

"Ok Hannah, I will do just that," replied the secretary.

As she settled at her desk, she made herself a cup of coffee to sip on while at her meeting. She grabbed the file and dashed into the meeting room.

The atmosphere in the meeting room was tense; both parties looking away from each other, trying hard not to make eye contact.

"Good morning, Mr. Raymond. How are you?"

Good morning, Barrister Hannah," he replied.

Hannah turned to Lisa, the single mother. "Good morning, Lisa. How are you and the children?"

"I am fine. The kids are both doing fine too. They are in school now. Thank you."

Hannah read the file again and asked if the landlord had changed his mind about taking Lisa to court.

He reluctantly answered, "After a long thought and because of the children, I will accept we settle out of court on the basis she will sort out a payment plan for the current accrued rent and the upcoming ones."

He turned to Lisa. "Can you do that?"

Lisa was about to talk when she felt the lump in her throat that came out as torrents of uncontrollable tears. Mr. Raymond felt so bad, and he said to her, "You know I am not a bad person but I need to pay my mortgage so my house will not be taken away from me. Please don't cry."

Hannah gave her some tissue to wipe her face. She wiped her face, blew her nose, and cleared her throat.

"I have spoken to the government who has promised to help. This will help me sort out how to pay all the money owed. I have also started looking for a job to help with all our bills."

Hannah felt God has helped her make this case easy. She filled the necessary documents and asked both parties to sign. She gave each a copy to keep. They both left happy. Hannah collected Lisa's number, promising to call her soon.

"Is there anything else I need to do?" asked Lisa.

"Oh yes. I would like to discuss something else with you."

"Ok, thank you. I will expect your call," Lisa replied.

Hannah felt a nudge from God that she should include Lisa and her children in the list of people she wanted to extend some help to.

She already had few people on the list she was already helping in her little way and she thought Lisa would need all the help she can get at this moment.

As Lisa left Hannah, thought "God you really have been good to me so much even as a single lady. Few years ago God instructed to not just waste her time waiting to be married but to start a charity.

It was funny at the time because all that occupied her thought is how to find a man and not be the last single standing "even though she knew she can never be the last single on earth"

She felt lonely and desperate that she always refuse to go out with her married friends or even the ones that are single like her.

She felt been single was a stigma even in the field she works, all the men do not accord her respect "or maybe that was her thought"

She feels if she's married maybe they will respect and appreciate all her cases that she has won.

So when she heard a word from God to start a charity she felt it was a ludicrous thing to do, for someone that is lonely and had decided to stay and wallow in her pain. But one thing she knows is that once God ask her to do something He will send all she need to accomplish it , and that was exactly what God did.

One day on her way to work she was in traffic when she had a knock on her window, she jumped as she turned to see who knocked on her window.

The sight brought her to tears, it a little boy who will not be more than 9 or 10 years old begging her to give him money.

She was stunned as she looked around to see if his parent where anywhere around. But there was no one around, the first thing she felt like doing was to pick him up and call the social services.

She decided no she will not do that, she motion the boy to follow her as she parked her car close to the pavement, as she was about to alight she saw the boy crying and about to walk away, she quickly alight and followed the boy toward an alley way.

At that moment she noticed a woman walking so quick the same direction with a baby in her hand.

It clicked that, the woman must be the boy's mother and seeing Hannah coming down from the car assume she was a social service staff. Hannah walked so fast that she caught up with the boy in two astride.

"Hi, little man" Hannah said

The boy had tears running down his face and pointing in the woman's direction saying mama mama.

Hannah tried to calm him down as she said " we will go after mama don't worry"

"what's your name?"

With tears in his eyes he said "Gerald"

At this point the woman stopped running and was looking from afar.

Hannah seized that time to talk to her, even though she wasn't sure if she can hear her but she kept talking,

"Hey mam, please wait"

"I just want to talk to you" My name is Hannah

At this point the woman took a few step

towards them, as Hannah kept talking.

"Are you ok?"

The woman said with tears in her eyes as she blubber out a few words "I am sorry, we just need some money to buy food"

Hearing that Hannah could not the tears. She told her to come closer, as she asked her a few questions.

Though this questions she was able to learn that the lady lost her husband a few years ago and because she didn't really know her husband's family and she was an orphan, she could not keep their house or get any jobs due to her still nursing a baby.

The government have not be able to help her out so she sleeps in an uncompleted building with the children.

Hannah helped her get the few belongings

they have, took her to an hotel and paid for a couple of night as she promised to come every day.

The next day she took her and her children for clothes shopping, after a few days she was able to rent her a small flat, Gerald was enrolled in school. That was how she start the charity God asked her to do.

One thing she noticed after registering and starting the charity properly was that she feels fulfilled and not lonely again. She takes the family out and sometimes they comes to her house to spend time with.

She realised this was the way God wanted to take her out of loneliness and desperation, she feels joy giving back to the community. Been married was not the only thing that can make you happy nor being single a disease.

Psalm 68:6

God sets the lonely in families, he leads out the prisoners with singing; but the rebellious live in a sun-scorched land.

God indeed gave her, her own family and she's so glad she got these ones to call family. She decided it is worth her waiting for her own husband and start a her own beautiful family.

Adding Lisa to the family is what God is telling her to do and she's happy to do it.

Chapter Five

Getting back to her office, she could not shake off the word God gave her in the car when she was thinking of Jonathan. She wondered what God was trying to tell her. God, is there something hidden that you want me to know about Jonathan? Have I jumped to a conclusion because of looks?

The intercom rang and as she picked it, the secretary's voice was heard saying there was a caller for her on the other line.

"Who is it?" she called from inside her office.

The secretary replied, "It's your mother." Hannah quickly checked her phone and realised her mother had called her like 5 times.

She had left her phone in her office when she went to the meeting room earlier; and coming back, she was too preoccupied that she didn't check her phone.

"Please put her through," Hannah said to the secretary.

With a sigh, she said, "Good morning mum, how are you?"

"I am fine, my darling. How are you too?"

"The Lord be praised," she replied. "Is everything ok? Is it not too early to call?" "Is it now a crime to call my daughter in the morning?"

"Oh, not at all, mum. I was just surprised."

"Anyway, I called to invite you to our church singles dinner program happening next Saturday.

I know you don't go out a lot these days but

locking yourself inside your house will not make you meet new people. You know what I mean by new people, right?"

Hannah was almost laughing out because she knew only husband related issue would make her mum call her this early. She also thought of telling her mum about Jonathan, but just as she was about to mention it, a lump formed in her throat and she could not bring the words out so she said the words that got out instead.

"Mum, can I get back to you later about the program? I will need to check my diary." "Ok, my darling. But I will love you to attend."

"How is dad?" She quickly interrupted her, hoping to stop her mum from talking further on the subject.

"Don't shut me up!" her mum interjected.

She continued, "Anyway, your dad is fine, still eating my food and making me happy, the way I will like your husband to be."

"Ok, mum. Let me call you later."

"Ok, bye. Love you. Talk later."

"Love you too, mum. Bye."

As her mum dropped the phone, she sat back thinking as she could feel the silence around her like a graveyard. Why does my mum always do this? I guess it's what all mothers do. They just want their children to marry and give them grandchildren.

Her hopes of introducing Jonathan to her so she could get her off her back looked so dim. Something in her felt it was not the right time or Jonathan was not the right one.

Thinking of it, in all the months they have

been together, Jonathan had never mentioned that he would like to meet her parents, and she didn't think she needed to push him. It was the right thing to do by him.

She snapped off her thoughts. I have work to do, instead of thinking of marriage stuff right now. It will surely happen in God's time

Chapter Six

Hannah was sitting by the window, slowly sipping her cup of coffee; her mind wondering what Jonathan was doing at the time. They were meant to go out on a dinner date this Saturday but Jonathan called to cancel, saying something urgent had come up and that he would be out of town.

She thought Jonathan cancelling their planned outings had now become a regular occurrence between them, and it was getting her worried. The more she looked at it, the more she felt there was something not right about their relationship. She was sure Jonathan was hiding something from her. She heard her phone ring. Reluctantly, she got up.

It was Sarah. "Good morning, Sarah. How are you?"

"I am fine. And you?"

"I hope you are not calling me because of mum's proposal for me to go for the singles program?" Hannah quickly asked.

Sarah laughed, "No, that's not why I am calling, though she also told me to convince you to go. Speaking of which, why didn't you tell her about Jonathan?"

"I don't know. I was going to, but I felt the Holy Spirit put a stop to my mouth." "That is the best decision. I am sure it was the Holy Spirit that stopped you." "And why is that?" asked Hannah.

Sarah hesitated but eventually gathered the courage to say what was on her mind.

"I recently noticed something that I feel I

need to let you know about Jonathan. I observed John stopped calling him and anytime I asked why he tried to ignore the question. This got me curious and uneasy about the drift in their relationship, especially with the way John constantly avoided my questions about him.

One night, I heard John on the phone with another friend of theirs and he was saying he was tired of Jonathan's lies about his business."

"Apparently, Jonathan had collected a lump sum of money from three of their friends, lying that he was in debt. I found this disturbing to hear as they know he is a recovering gambler and there were chances of him getting back into gambling."

"I was furious that I jumped in on their

conversation. I was not happy John never told me Jonathan was a recovering gambler. He also never expressed his concerns about him to me whenever I asked. He apologized, saying he wanted to be sure before telling me. He also said that was why he was reluctant to connect you and Jonathan, though Jonathan had been clean for a few years and we didn't think there was anything to be afraid of. Now everyone is concerned, but at the same time, not sure."

Hannah stayed quiet, listening to Sarah's narration. Her mind, however, flashed back to her prayer last night, when she fervently asked God to reveal any hidden secret about Jonathan. "Are you there?" Sarah asked.

"Oh, sorry. I am here," Hannah responded. Hannah told Sarah her concerns about

Jonathan and how he has been acting lately.

"My first concern was whenever I speak about God; he tries to avoid the conversation. Then lately he has been cancelling our date outings at short notice.

There was a day I was thinking about him and God gave me a bible verse that has made me pray more about him."

"I am glad the Holy Spirit warned me to be careful and pray more regarding the relationship, and since then I have noticed him change even more and more."

Sarah said to her, "Please Hannah, be careful."

"I will, sis," replied Hannah. "How is my angel? I miss her so much. Hopefully, I can have her come over for a sleepover soon."

"She will be ecstatic. She has been singing

that into my ears for a while. Just let me know the weekend you want her so John and I can go for a weekend break too."

"Ok, will do, once I check my diary."

"So, are you going to the singles program?"

Hannah laughed, "You are becoming like mum; but sorry to disappoint you, I am not going. I am tired of these single programs. It is full of young girls and guys, and always the same topic. I am tired of them. I am thinking of going to the cinema with Sandra. I called her and she's up for it."

"Ok then, enjoy your day. I will talk to you soon. Love you"

"Love you too. Talk soon. Give my angel my love. Let her know auntie misses her and I will come and pick her soon.

Chapter Seven

The days and weeks felt like they were draggy. Hannah had been feeling feverish for a few days now, and she thought it contributed to the sluggish feeling. She even had to stay at home from work.

The doorbell rang, and Hannah was too tired to get to the door. The person at the door was insistent and was not giving up anytime soon. Hannah dragged herself to the door, and through the peephole, she saw Jonathan.

She leaped as she has not heard from him for some weeks. She opened the door and said hello as she managed to drag herself back to her seat.

"Hi Hannah, How are you?"

"I've not been too well. I'm feeling a little better now. You?"

"I am okay. Sorry I have not called for a while. I have been so busy." "Really? Too busy to even send a text?" replied Hannah.

"I know I should have called, but I could not get to my phone. But I am here now."

Hannah was going to say more, but something stopped her from talking. She changed the conversation and asked if he would like something to drink. Jonathan said no that he just came to check on her briefly and he needed to go somewhere asap.

Hannah thought this was the opportunity for her to find out his stand on Christ since she doesn't know when next she will see him.

The past year had been an off-and-on

relationship with him.

She was tired of the relationship and needed to know where it was going. No more time-wasting.

"I have been meaning to ask you a question, but never found the right time to ask."

"You can ask me now," replied Jonathan.

At that moment, Hannah noticed he went pale and looked scared, but she ignored his facial expressions.

I wanted to ask, "Are you born again?"

She noticed the lines of relief on his face and wondered what he thought she was going to ask. Jonathan looked away and stood up. After a while, he turned to Hannah. "I am sorry to disappoint you, Hannah. I don't believe in those religious things."

Hannah turned red and looked shocked.

Though she knew Jonathan avoided discussions about Christ, she never thought he could be an atheist. She was almost crying. Out of all the guys she had come in contact with, even in the church, how had she picked an atheist?

Hannah replied, trying to maintain calm despite the heavy hurt she felt inside. "Why didn't you tell me? And you know my stand about my belief!"

Jonathan lashed out. "The reason I said nothing is because I am tired of you, Christians. You think you are better than other people. You act as if you know it all and every other person is an idiot. I am sick and tired of you people!" His eyes turned red, and he looked as if he was going to attack her.

Hannah knew she had to be careful since

she was alone with him. She muttered a prayer under her breath, asking God to protect and deliver her from this monster she chose amongst others.

Hannah turned to him and politely asked him to leave. Jonathan turned to her and spewed, "Good riddance to bad rubbish. I am tired of your church life, anyway. I wanted to see how far you will go before realising I was only in this relationship to prove that church girls too can fall for an atheist and not know!"

He stormed out the door and slammed it.

Hannah was tired of guys saying you church girl, Just because a Girl will not do things that does not glorify God or that are not moral.

Or you decided to be disciplined and different from other doesn't mean you are proving difficult.

Hannah was relieved and thanked God he didn't hurt her. What would she have done? She could barely move, not to talk of a fight. She looked up with tears in her eyes and said "Thank you, Lord." She closed her eyes as a bible verse came to her.

She quickly grabbed her bible to read what it says, as she always relied on hearing God talk to her through this means.

John 1:17 "For the law was given through Moses, but grace and truth came through Jesus Christ."
As she meditated on the verse, she realized God through His unfailing love had kept her from a dangerous relationship that would have led to her destruction, and by His faithfulness; he revealed the truth to her.

A clearer revelation of the bible verse in

Jeremiah 5:14 God gave ages ago regarding Jonathan now made sense to her.

God did put fire in her mouth through her prayer, thereby revealing the person of Jonathan. She hoped the bridge that connected them was completely burnt.

She felt she needed to speak to someone. Sarah might be the best person to speak to right now. She dialled Sarah's number, and as she picked she shouted,

"Hannah, are you ok? I was just about to call you."

Hannah was surprised because she purposely didn't call her or any of her family to tell them she was sick.

"Are you alright, Sarah?"

"Yes, I am. Have you heard?"

"Heard what?" Hannah replied.

"About Jonathan, what happened to him?"

At this point, Hannah was confused and was wondering what Sarah was saying. "Jonathan just left my place, and that's why I am calling you."

Sarah shouted, "Are you safe? Did he do anything to you? Did he take anything from you?"

Hannah interjected, "Sarah, please calm down. What are you saying?"

"John just received a call from a friend that said Jonathan was on the run from the police. He has been charged for drug peddling, fraud, and money laundering. His house has been surrounded, but he was not home when they came."

Hannah was speechless, "Are you kidding me right now?! Jonathan just left my house angrily because I asked him about his Christian faith, and he told me he is an atheist and was only with me to prove a point!"

Sarah said, "Thank God he didn't hurt you, and at least he's gone for good. I hope the police will not see your number on his phone and come for you. I am sorry for making you meet this guy."

"Oh, please don't be sorry. I accepted his hand in a relationship without seeking God's opinion.

I just thank God nothing sexual transpired between us. I think I am tired of being desperate to get married.

From now on, I will enjoy my life, go on more outings with friends and wait on God to bring the right man."

"That's good, but I trust mummy will still

be on your neck," said Sarah. "Don't worry, I know how to handle her," replied Hannah.

Chapter Eight

It's a sunny and bright morning, the birds are chirping, the trees are clapping and swaying as though bowing to their creator.
The ambience seemed so perfect you could bet it was going to be a good day.

Hannah sat by the TV sipping on her morning brewed cup of coffee. She never missed this morning routine.

It was her perfect companion. She decided to turn the TV on for a bit of news and information on current global happenings. As she selected the news channel, the Breaking News highlight jumped out at her.

The presenter's voice immediately followed, "The world is sent into chaos as a virus that has no cure is aggressively ravaging the world and scientists are afraid it's affecting and killing people quicker than they can control.

Scientists and Medical experts do not know much about its genetic materials yet. The Government is confused about this. No solution appears to be in sight."

As Hannah glided through several other channels and all she heard was the same. Time seems to be running out.

People are generating theories and different forms of treatments which have not been tested nor confirmed to be a reliable cure are being introduced to individuals.

After weeks of a failed attempt to find the cure to this global pandemic, the global government has resorted to enforcing a national lockdown too, at the very least, contain the virus.

People are being asked to limit physical interactions, regularly wash their hands after touching surfaces, avoid touching their faces, and restrain from hugging and handshaking.

A lot of investigations have gone into this raging pandemic and there have been several findings. The pandemic was said to have started in China with a lot of deaths and casualties.

Different theories are surfacing. Some are saying it is 5G related, some others think it's the world coming to an end.

The summary of it all was an immediate lockdown as ordered by the government, businesses are to be shut down, places of worship closed, local and international travels were to be on hold.

The world was shutting down basically, leaving the internet, social media, and telephone calls as the only means of communication.

Phew! Hannah sighed. This was a lot to take in. All that clouded her mind was how this would affect her job, her almost non-existent social life, and most importantly her faith in God. Worshipping at her church was a thing she held so dearly – she was clearly pained.

For a while now she had felt she was the only single person in church in her age bracket.

This made it difficult for her to get fully involved in the Singles' Department. Every other single were in their 20s and still having fun. They didn't seem so desperate to get married.

The only other older single person in the church was Sister Mary, who had been in an off-and-on relationship with Brother James in the choir. One minute you saw them together, the next minute you would hear her rant about how men are not good and don't know what they want.

Hannah felt like she didn't belong in most of the groups in the church. Almost everyone was married.

She did not allow this to affect her dedication to serving God, though.

She had decided to keep trusting and waiting on God for the right man; hoping he would walk into the church or that their paths would cross on the day she went out.

Now the worst news was being broadcasted on TV.

Amid that ominous feeling threatening to overwhelm her, she decided to have her Nature and Bible study time - a habit she loved doing on Saturdays. She took her Bible with her to her balcony and opened it. (She usually just opens any page in the bible and meditates on any verse that jumps out to her).

The verse she got today *was Luke 1:37: "For with God nothing shall be impossible."*

As she meditated on this word, she felt a flow of peace through her vein.

In the same second, another feeling crept in and she thought, God how will you make it happen for me? You promised to divinely locate me with my partner. How would that happen with this new ban on physical interactions? The Word she had read in the bible however kept re-echoing in her mind and she concluded that if God had said it, then with Him nothing truly shall be impossible. She continued to sip her coffee and silently praying.

As the days rolled into another, the news of increasing death rates and numbers of infected persons spread like wildfire; and just like the Biblical saying, men's hearts truly began to fail them for fear.

However, for Hannah, the Word she got in the Scriptures kept resonating in her mind and with it, she was able to maintain some calm and find strength in these unprecedented times.

At bedtime, she meditated on Psalms 91:1-

16 and she sensed another word from God for her. To her, these would be her anchor scriptures for as long as the pandemic would last. The verses from that text gave her a soothing assurance that God would hide her and her family in His pavilion, in His secret place where no harm would come to them.

She could almost literally feel the wind of peace blowing through her house, and her heart and mind were filled with a river of peace. The one that trusts God will always be at peace. With this in her mind, she prayed and went to bed.

With the new 'lockdown' normal, staying still to fellowship with God through His word had now become a regular practice.

It used to be her Saturday routine before the lockdown but the new normal made it a nearly everyday practice – and she loved to have it right on her balcony.

One lovely day as she settled to have her time of fellowship, her phone rang. She wondered who it could be as she had spoken with her parents and siblings the previous night.

To add to her puzzled state, the Caller ID on her phone screen read Private. With a bit of hesitation, she tapped the receiver button and a male voice on the other end said "Hello!"

Hannah was surprised to hear a male and unfamiliar voice but she responded with a more courteous "Hello" hoping to recognise the voice.

The male voice at the other end said, "Good morning ma'am. How are you today?

How are you coping with the pandemic? I hope you're keeping safe too?"

Hannah was still somewhat lost as the man was yet to introduce himself neither was his voice any familiar.

She composed herself, with firmness in her voice, "I'm fine and keeping safe, thank God. May I know who this is, please?"

The voice at the other end answered, "Pardon my insolence. My name is Adam. I worship with the local assembly downtown.

We are currently running a love initiative where we make random calls to people especially in these unstable times. We extend our arms of love and care by checking on them and helping with groceries and food, where necessary. Your number was the first I clicked on this morning, so… here we are!

How are you keeping, ma'am?" he wrapped up his mini speech with a smile in his voice.

This made Hannah relax a bit as she let out her response with some air of relief escaping through her lips, "I'm very well, thank you. I'm doing my best to keep safe as well.

I really appreciate this initiative and I'm certain it would be a blessing to a lot of persons like me."

Hannah's mood immediately shifted from feeling dejected and alone to feeling remembered by God because how else could she explain how her number had been selected to be called by this church group at this particular time she was feeling lonely. She got the message clearly. God is with me. I am not alone.

The sound of Adam's warm voice jolted her

back to reality, "Feel free to let me know if you'd need any supplies and I'd inform the church to get them across to you."

Hannah was still in shock and awe of God. She muttered a few words to Adam that she was fine and would not have need of anything.

For her, the fact that God remembered her was worth more than the supplies offered. She said her thanks and goodbye.

Chapter Nine

As Adam dropped the phone, he felt a sense of connection to this woman he just spoke with. She had only said a few words but he felt like he had found a friend in this person.

Volunteering for initiatives in the church was not usually his thing but he was pleased with himself for not ignoring this opportunity when it came.

He quickly scribbled her number so as not to forget. Adam could not wait to give her another call just so he could hear her voice again.

Over the past couple of days, he had interacted with dozens of persons but he wondered why this particular call stood out for him.

He said a few prayers for her and for all the people he has called since the beginning of the initiative and for the people he would still call.

He was full of thanks for the privilege to be a breath of fresh air to the people he had interacted with.

Some of them were living in fear – the kind of fear that made you automatically feel ill. Some were grieving family members lost to the pandemic.

A young man in his late twenties was just on the verge of suicide before Adam's call came in. With constant check-up calls, words of encouragement, food, and inspiring books made available to him, he was able to break free from the downward spiral of depression.

The church even provided him with a laptop so he could connect to uplifting messages and watch movies.

The other day he got to call him again, he could hear the sound of hope and joy in his voice. These experiences encouraged him to do more.

This first call he made today had really brightened his mood. The lady sounded polite and he guessed she was a Christian.

He could feel the peace even in the few words she spoke. She sounded like she had everything under control and needed no help but he sensed the urge to call her again. Something in her voice makes me want to call her again.

Asides from the calm he felt in her voice, he was sure he heard her say 'Thank God' just before the line got disconnected.

Only a person who truly knows God would maintain such a level of peace in this pandemic, he thought.

He had planned to call five persons today so he could focus on his office to-do list ahead of him. He picked his phone and proceeded to dial the next number.

Hannah sat back in her balcony, wondering what coincidence it was that, out of the blues, a man with a soothing, solemn, and lovely voice would call her in the middle of this loneliness she felt so strongly in her life right now.

She didn't even know when she let out a loud laugh. She found it ridiculous! Like… When was the last time I had a man call to check up on me? Though Adam had called based on an instruction from church, she refused to dismiss it as mere coincidence. She strongly felt God saying something through all of it. One sure message she was getting was that no matter the situation, when you think all hope is gone, God can still show up. She silently prayed that he calls again.

The hours went by so fast and soon it was night. The moon was already seen beautifully brightening the gradually darkened night.

Hannah sat by the fireplace with a book in hand to calm her brain. As she opened to continue from where she had left off, her mind drifted to the morning caller again, Adam.

There has to be something about this guy. She couldn't wait to figure it out.

It was as though her heart skipped a beat

every time she thought of him. She also realised she did not know anything about him and would not want to sound too forward by calling him. Then it dawned on her that she did not even have his number. She had to stay hopeful that he would call again and soon.

Adam had been staring at his phone wondering if calling now was a good idea. What if she thinks I'm crazy? What if I'm disturbing her? What if she's married with children and my call causes a rift between them? What if she doesn't want to talk to me? What if? What if? All these thoughts kept flooding his mind.

He finally gathered the courage as he picked the phone and dialled Hannah's number.

As the phone rang continuously, his mind raced. He was going to drop the call at the fifth ring when he heard 'Hello' from the other side. His heart jumped.

He also didn't know if to drop the call or say something. He decided to speak.

"Hello ma'am, this is Adam again." He kept quiet then went on, "I am the guy who called you in the morning. How are you and the family?" He hurriedly spat the words from his mouth, then he decided to calm down so she would not notice he was shaking.

He continued "I felt our first conversation was awkward so I decided to call again tonight." Although in his mind, all he knew he wanted was to hear her voice.

When Hannah heard the phone ring, her heart jumped. Could it be him or someone else? Isn't it too quick for him to call again? How do I compose myself to talk to him if he is the one calling? How do I hide my excitement from my voice? As the phone continued to ring, her thoughts ran a marathon. She eventually decided to pick up.

She said "hello" and could feel the silence like a knife cutting the air so much that if a pin dropped, she was sure to hear it as loud as a hurricane. She said "hello" again and the voice on the other side came through.

Chapter Ten

Adam finally composed himself and said hello again. He decided to introduce himself properly and slowly this time. He repeated, "My name is Adam. How are you and the family?" He chipped in the family part. He thought that would make her want to listen. By now, Hannah had gathered composure and she replied, telling him how the day had started great and she was certain it would finish well too. On second thought, she thought she was being too casual with a man she barely knew. She however decided to take a bold step by engaging Adam in a chat. She asked him why he chose to participate in this random call initiative.

Adam immediately seized the opportunity to talk to the lady he's suddenly grown fond of. "My name is Adam Williams. I work for a company called Hedgecart Ltd where we help small income businesses invest in bigger companies so they can grow and expand. We also major in Construction and Real Estate." We are building a new headquarters here in UK, as our main branch is in US, but with the growing of the company we thought it will be a good idea to extend our branch to Europe; UK been our first stop. And the hammer fell on me to come and start the branch. Adam wrapped up what seemed like a basic profile of himself.

He continued, "You also asked why I volunteered to join the random call initiative. Well, I would say it was a divine instruction for me.

When our church (My family church here in UK) announced its plan to do something godly and different in this season that can bring joy to people in lockdown and at home, I sensed God ministering to me through His Word *in Jeremiah 50:34: "Their Redeemer is strong; The Lord of hosts is His name. He will thoroughly plead their case that He may give rest to the land, and disquiet the inhabitants of Babylon."* I got the understanding that God was about to bring rest to the land in this time of chaos. We were given a list of numbers to randomly call and prayerfully select the people who need the supplies to be distributed to. I was given 20 numbers and yours was the 17th I called."

Hannah interrupted him, "So do you call the same number twice?"

Adam was caught off guard. He replied, "Not really but we leave our church administrator's number and if they do need anything, they can call the office."

Hannah interrupted again while trying not to sound rude, "So why didn't you leave the administrator's number when you first called, and why are you calling back by yourself?"

Adam felt a bit of fear but he summoned courage and replied, "Since the first time I called, something in me tells me you will be a friend to keep."

At this point, Hannah cuts in, "Please can we continue this conversation again tomorrow? I have a prayer meeting in a few minutes and would like to prepare before we start."

Adam replied, "Okay, that's fine. Thank you

for talking with me. Goodnight." "Thank you too. Goodnight," she responded.

Chapter Eleven

As Hannah dropped the call she looked up to God and asked, "God what do you want from me in this situation?" The Spirit dropped a verse in her heart in Obadiah 1:17 "But on Mount Zion there shall be [a]deliverance, And there shall be holiness; The house of Jacob shall possess their possessions. She pondered on the verse; several thoughts kept racing through her mind.

Has God finally heard my cry and sent help to me? Or am I just over analysing the situation? Regardless of how things would eventually turn out, she believed what God was saying and she was certain that what was hers would come to her.

She dialled her prayer group number and connected to the ongoing prayer session while meditating on the Bible verse God had just given her. As she listened to the person leading the prayer session, she felt a flood of peace flow through her.

Adam stared at the wall. He couldn't hide the excitement from hearing Hannah's voice again. A part of him still wondered if she was single and searching.

He felt God telling him this was the lady He had made him wait for. He had tried to be friendly with some sisters in the church, but the connection he felt when he spoke with Hannah was strong and peaceful.

He closed his eyes and a Word came to his mind. *Ezekiel 48:35: "All the way around shall be eighteen thousand cubits; and the name of the city from that day shall be: THE[a] LORD IS THERE."* With the last line 'The Lord is There' resonating in his mind, he prayed more, got up to get a cup of coffee and let out a deep breath. Tomorrow is another day.

The droplets of rain on the ceiling woke Hannah up. She looked at the clock and realised she had been sleeping on the sofa for 4hrs. She walked to the window, staring as the rain droplets slid down the window pane.

She marvelled at the work of God, and how soothing the rain feels when it pours. She also wondered at the awesomeness of God to bring a great harvest when the rain waters the plants. She got lost in her thoughts again.

If only we all can allow the rain of God to fall on our thoughts, maintaining our peace, and knowing that if He promised it, He will surely do it. Her thoughts drifted to Adam.

She was particularly in awe of how God could bring someone into her life, and not only that, cause her to feel an emotion she had never experienced before. Adam's deep yet melodic voice was one she was sure she wanted to hear again. She found herself unconsciously guessing if he was tall or short, light or dark, sporty or on the big side, by his voice.

She jumped out of her thoughts immediately as she thought that wasn't a godly thing to do. What if he's married with children? The thought of that definitely brought a bittersweet feeling. She closed the curtain, went into her bedroom, and drifted back to sleep.

Adam held Hannah's hand as they walked

by the sea, smiling and excited with each other, enjoying the air as it caressed their bodies without interfering with their peaceful and loving moment. Adam's face shone in the sunshine as he felt God had finally answered his prayer by giving him a woman as beautiful and loving as Hannah. He was about to kiss her when he heard his phone ring only to realise it was a dream. He jumped up, picked his phone as he recognised the number as his pastor's.

"Good morning, Brother Adam. I'm sorry I woke you up. Can you talk?" Adam replied in the affirmative as he rubbed the sleep off his eyes. He checked the time. It was 10 am. He had overslept. He usually woke up at 7 am. He must have stayed up so late last night thinking about Hannah.

The pastor continued, "I had a dream today. God asked me to tell you about it and to pray with you. I saw you in a luscious garden with lots of lovely flowers. A lovely pink one stood out among them. It was different from the others. It was a

beautiful pink with white dots on its petals. Then I saw you going round the garden oblivious of this one beautiful flower that stood out. Every second you glanced at it you always looked away thinking if you looked too much, the flower may die. At one corner stood the gardener waiting and expecting you to ask him about the pink flower. He even offered to sell it to you as he thought that flower should be the first to be noticed by anyone, but you did not pay as much attention to it.

While in the dream, a word came to me in *2 Chronicles 26:5 "Uzziah followed God in the time of Zechariah's life. Zechariah taught Uzziah how to respect and obey God. When Uzziah was obeying the Lord, God gave him success."* I also heard in my spirit, My son come to me and ask that I may tell you the secret you need which rhymes with this verse in *Psalms 25: 14: "The Lord tells his secrets to his followers. He teaches them about his agreement."* And I woke up."

"Brother Adam, I pray God opens your heart as He explains this dream to you. Is it ok if I pray with you?"

Adam obliged.

The pastor said a prayer and ended the conversation, leaving Adam in thoughts.

Chapter Twelve

Hannah walked outside to get some fresh air and to check on her garden. She noticed a few tomatoes coming out. She was excited. As she picked some weeds around the plants, she felt a nudge to pray a simple prayer, "God, the world is on lockdown but you did not hold back from causing this plant to grow. It means nothing can stop you when you decide to bless.

God, please send your blessings to me even when I least expect them. Amen." As she finished, she heard her phone ring.

She had left it on the patio table. Wondering who it might be, she dusted her hand on her garden clothes and went for the phone.

"Hi Hannah," came the familiar voice of her sister.

Hannah replied, "Hey! How are you? I was planning to call you and mum later today. How are my blessed niece and nephew?"

Her sister, Sarah answered "We are fine. Trust you are well too. Hope you are keeping safe and not feeling lonely. I was thinking about you this morning when this word came to me in *Isaiah 54:7 "For a short time I turned away from you, but with all my love I will welcome you again."* I just felt the need to call and encourage you. Though this lockdown is a peculiar time where we have nowhere to go and no one to visit, God said to let you know that He would surprise you even in this season.

Always remember we are a phone call away and you can always call me anytime."

Hannah said her thanks and began to tell her sister about the strange man who called her. They both joked and had a good laugh over it. It felt good telling her sister about it. She hardly ever keeps a secret from her sister.

They always talk about everything whether good or bad. She was her number one cheerleader.

Sarah called the children to come and speak with their special aunt. They were giddy with excitement as it had been a while since they last saw or spoke with their aunt. She overheard them screaming her name and making a fuss over who would speak first.

Thinking of how to manage the frenzy, she went, "Hey, darlings, the elder one talks first, remember!"

Charlotte shouted to Timothy, "You see! I am the elder one and I get to talk first!"

Timothy reluctantly said, "Ok, you win."

This worked all the time. Charlotte was the chatty one. After all the pleasantries, she asked, "Auntie when are you getting married so you can have someone to live with you so you won't have to be alone in the house."

Hannah chuckled, "Soon, my darling."

Charlotte let out an excited, "Yaayyyy!!!" and joyfully gave the phone to Timothy.

Timothy began his own round of questioning. "When are we coming to your house?" "Do you know when the lockdown will end so I can come for a sleepover?" "I miss your food and your sweet cake pops."

"Don't worry, it will end soon." Hannah

tried to pacify him. "I definitely miss our sleepovers too".

Hannah did some more small talk with her sister and ended the call.

She went to have one more look at her budding tomato plants while deep in thoughts, "God when?! I know you have promised me so I have confidence that if you have said it, you will bring it to pass. I believe your word in *Hosea 14:9 "A wise person understands these things and a smart person should learn them. The Lord's ways are right. Good people will live by them. Sinners will die by them."* I know the words are for me and I know your ways are right. I will follow you and hold on to your promise for me knowing your promise never fails. Thank you, God."

Hannah walked back into her house, had a

shower, dressed up, and went into the kitchen to make herself something to eat. As she prepared the food, she thought of Adam. In her imagination, she saw him as being tall, handsome, and God-fearing. She wanted to speak with him again but didn't want to be the one to make the first call. It was a sunny day so she took her food to the patio. She grabbed her bible on the way. As she munched on her food, she decided to open her bible as usual for a word to meditate on. She was led to *Isaiah 18:4 The Lord said, "I will be in the place prepared for me. I will quietly watch these things happen: On a beautiful summer day, at noon, people will be resting. (It will be during the hot harvest time when there is no rain, but only early morning dew.)"* God, according to this verse, I have decided to rest in you for all I need and wait for. I know you will definitely provide. I will not be too desperate or impatient to walk away from your promise and end up backsliding.

As she meditated on the word, her phone rang. She leaped both with fear and joy as she looked at it. She could recognise the number as Adam's. She picked at the third ring trying to keep her excitement under check. She muffled a "hello" as Adam began to talk. She could sense a bit of shyness in his voice that she had not heard or felt before.

She went on to ask him how he was keeping up in the lockdown. Almost immediately after he responded, she followed up with the question, "Are you married?"

She had blurted out the question before realising it and made to 'correct' herself, "I actually meant how are you and your family, your wife and children inclusive."

The silence on the other end of the line was deafening. After a few minutes, Adam composed himself to speak. He had not expected Hannah to be bold enough to pop up the question especially as he was scared to ask her too.

Hannah heard his response after what felt like an eternity, "I am not married. I also do not have children yet. I stay alone and I'm keeping safe in the Lord. Thank you for asking."

Adam decided to use this moment to ask her the same question. He blurted it out quickly before he lost the courage, "And you?"

Hannah knew the question would come and

she was ready to answer. She responded, "Just like you, I am not married. I also don't have children." They both laughed.

Adam then requested to know a bit about her.

She attempted a brief introduction, "My name is Hannah Daniels, the last child of a family of 6 siblings. I am a Christian and work as a lawyer for a law firm." She thought that was enough information to give out for now.

Adam carried on the conversation, "Can I ask what you do as a pastime in this period of lockdown?"

"I have been writing a book I started prior to the lockdown. I also enjoy tending to my garden.

These help me ward off any feelings of boredom when they come creeping in."

Hannah chuckled as she chatted away.

Adam liked the feeling he felt while talking with Hannah. He could tell she was relaxed and felt comfortable speaking to him. He warmed up more and also filled Hannah in with all he had been up to during the lockdown.

He let her in on his work-from-home schedule, how he spends his free time watching movies, and everything in between.

They talked for a long time, oblivious of how fast time went by. By the time they both looked at the time, they had been on the phone for 3 hours! Reluctantly, Adam told Hannah he had to go catch up with some important tasks.

Chapter Thirteen

As Hannah dropped the call, a sense of peace she could not explain flushed through her. She always felt this peace every time she spoke with this 'stranger'. She really could not understand the feeling but she felt somewhat sure that something had come out of the lockdown eventually.

One more thing: now she was doubly sure she wasn't hitting on another woman's husband and most importantly, he was single! Her face broke into a shy smile.

Back at home, Adam felt like jumping, dancing, and singing praises after the call.

For him, the greatest achievement was the

realisation that Hannah was single. All his fears have been removed.

He immediately began to toy with the idea of asking her out already. That would have been the next step to take if not for the lockdown restrictions.

Almost in the same minute, he thought of Sister Dorothy in the church who had been warming up to him lately though he didn't think he was attracted to her.

On a counter thought, this new lady; How do you even get attracted to someone you've never met? I don't know what she looks like. How do I ask her out? What do I say? The questions hit him back to back!

He decided that the next step would be to ask for a picture of her. He was too worried about being labelled as too forward.

He didn't want to soil this new budding friendship they seemed to be building. He knows a few ladies in the church, so he knew fairly well how sensitive ladies can be when they sense an intrusion into their private life.

He tried to distract himself from thinking too hard about Hannah but thoughts of her flooded his mind the rest of the day. Lord, is this from you or merely some infatuation?

He had waited too long and did not want to make a mistake in the end. He decided to pray in that moment.

As he knelt, a word came to him in *Acts 1:26: "Then they used lots to choose one of the two men. The lots showed that Matthias was the one the Lord wanted. So he became an apostle with the other eleven."* Adam found that passage rather confusing. He unconsciously voiced out his thoughts, "But God, I don't want to cast a lot concerning the woman that will be my future wife.

All I ask is that you show me exactly who my wife is. I never want to make the wrong choice."

As he prayed, the Holy Spirit dropped *Psalms 32:8 in his heart. "The Lord says, I will teach you and guide you in the way you should live. I will watch over you and be your guide."*

That passage was all the assurance he needed. He was sure God would lead him on the right path and right decision.

He had always lived his life on God and had been directed by God's Word. This has worked for him even in the toughest times. God never ceased to show up for him. While lost in his thoughts, a particular scenario of

God's faithfulness flashed through his mind.

It was the day God called him. He felt all hope was lost. He had just lost his job. The house he was living in he could not pay his rent so he has to turn to the Council for a house beneath his living standard.

He could not bear to tell his family of his struggles. The lady he was in a relationship with left him because of his financial status at the time.

One day, he had decided to end it all when he got a call from his mother to expect a call from an old friend.

Adam's old friend had just moved to the area with his family. Coincidentally, they had chosen Adam's family church as their place of worship and met Adam's mum in service that evening. He requested Adam's number as he had lost it. Adam's mum was calling that night informing him to expect a call from his friend.

Adam reconnected with his friend after a few days and they decided to meet at a major spot in town for dinner. They had a great conversation that night which turned out to be the start of a glorious turnaround in Adam's life. His friend was able to help him get back on his feet financially. He also led him to Christ and since then, he's recorded impressive growth in his life. Adam remained grateful to God for bringing his friend back to his life and for accepting him with all his flaws.

He moved over to US to start afresh and God was good to him as he was able build an empire for himself, and now he's seeing expansion in different part of the world.

Psalm 2:8 Ask of Me, and I will give You The nations for Your inheritance, And the ends of the earth for Your possession. He now serves in his local church and makes himself available for God's service. Moving back to UK temporarily has also saw him back in his family church; the same church he was christened and grew up in. He made up his mind wherever he is he will serve God.

Chapter Fourteen

Hannah woke up to the sound of her alarm. She needed to continue the book that she had been writing for too long a time now. The book was taking too long, she's not a writer but really wanted to write this, but most times she get writer's block (as they call it), but she was determined to write this book and hopefully finish during this lockdown.

She got up, observed her morning devotion and quiet time. When she finished, she made herself a cup of coffee. This was her drill whenever she needed to do some writing. The taste had a way of increasing her alertness level in the morning. She already had decided on the book title.

All she needed was to get started writing. She had procrastinated a lot and hoped that the lockdown would spur her to write.

As she picked up her notebook and pen, her mind drifted again to Adam. This had been recurring the past few weeks. She thought, God why do I always feel joy every time I think of him? She was however thankful she had found a friend in this lockdown and was hopeful he would be one to keep.

She was looking forward to his call later today as he had promised to call in the evening.

Hannah pulled her thoughts back to her book. Her book was about an old woman who decided to tell her life history from her childhood, teenage years through to adulthood, and old age. It's a fictional story plot that jumped at her the last time she went to her grandmother's.

One of her grandmother's friends had visited and they were reliving old times as friends. This made her want to write a book highlighting the life experiences of the elderly. She always loved to hear her grandmother tell her stories of her life as a young girl. The plan was to compile a memoir of those stories while she was still alive.

The sound of the telephone ringing gave Adam a startle. He wasn't expecting any call this early except it was work-related.

"Hello. How may I help you?" Adam spoke into the phone trying to figure out who the caller was.

"Good morning, Sir. My name is Bradley,

calling from A&G Company. You put in a contract bid with us before the lockdown. I have been asked to call to let you know that the contract has been approved for you. The board has also decided to double the amount you asked for knowing that once the lockdown is lifted, the prices of the material needed for the project would have increased."

Adam was completely speechless. Bradley continued, "We want to find out if you can commence the project once the lockdown is lifted."

Adam stuttered a "Yes, we can."

Bradley then asked, "Can you please send us an email confirmation so we can return the signed contract to you?"

Adam replied, still in disbelief, "Okay, do expect it before noon. Thank you and goodbye."

As he dropped the phone trying to come to terms with the contract just awarded to him, his mobile phone rang. He reluctantly picked the phone. It was Scott, his PA at the office.

"Good morning, Adam. Kindly accept my sincere apologies for calling this early. I just got some news too good to keep to myself."

Adam replied almost immediately, "Good news?! Please tell me! Surprisingly, I have good news for you too."

Scott continued, "Do you remember the contract bid we sent to Diamond Communications that we thought we had lost? I got an email from them this morning to say we've been awarded the contract!"

Adam could not contain his joy as he screamed, "Thank you, Jesus!!!" He gave his own good news to Scott and asked him to send an email to management letting them know there is work to be done once the lockdown is lifted, hopefully soon.

One thing Adam always ensured as the CEO was for everyone to be involved in the affairs of the company.

When there was good news or less good news, everyone gets to hear about it. They all work together like a family, creating a friendly and warm ambience for work.

They observe the Open Office policy. This has worked very well for the company as members of staff are free to share ideas to enhance the company. Staff's personal issues and overall wellbeing are also always catered to.

Adam was so excited he didn't realise he

had dialled Hannah's number immediately after dropping the call with Scott.

Before he could stop the ringing, he heard Hannah's "Hello!"

He returned the hello and was about to apologise for calling this early when Hannah interrupted, "I wasn't expecting your call this early. I hope everything is fine."

Adam responded, "Oops! I'm sorry to disturb you. I was just too happy and your number was the one I thought to dial."

Hannah said, "That's fine, I was up already. So what's the reason for this early morning joy?"

Adam responded excitedly, "God just showed His awesomeness in my life. Not that His blessings are new in my life, but in this year of the pandemic when everyone seems to be experiencing casting down, all I can say is, God is lifting the company up. There are these two contracts we submitted before the lockdown. They are both huge contracts we have really been looking forward to.

I got a call this morning that both have been approved. One of them came back with even double the quote we gave them!"

"Praise God!" Hannah burst out.

Adam responded, "It's a miracle and I am so happy."

"God will bring many more your company's way."

Adam said, "Amen. Thank you." He felt his spirit overflowing with joy.

The lockdown had truly been a time of lifting up for him. Adam was so happy he made the right choice by calling Hannah.

"I am sorry for disturbing your morning. I hope this doesn't negate my call later," he added with a smile in his voice.

Hannah laughed out loud, "No, you can still call me later. It was nice to share in your joy."

Chapter Fifteen

Hannah stared at the phone after dropping the call. It definitely feels different with this man. She was happy he found it easy to share his good news with her even though they barely knew each other. She sighed, my faceless friend. She turned to focus on her book which she had only managed to write halfway of chapter one.

Adam put the phone down, thinking to himself. What did I just do? Why did I call her? Of all the people to share this pleasant news with, I could have called mum.

She's always praying for my business to expand. Or I could have called my sister who

I even promised to call this morning.

He looked up and muttered, "God, are you telling me something?" His mind wandered again to Hannah's sweet voice as she prayed for him and how she laughed so lovingly. This lady must be special.

It was getting dark. Hannah had just had her dinner. She looked at the phone for the 10th time, wondering why Adam had not called as promised. Or should she call? Will that be alright? Will it not project me as being desperate? Why has he not called? Just as she stood up to take her plates to the kitchen, the phone rang.

She almost dropped her plates in fright. She quickly composed herself so as not to sound too excited.

She still allowed the phone to ring two more

times before picking though, trying hard to conceal her excitement.

"Good evening, how are you?" Adam said to her. "I am sorry for calling late. I had a family zoom meeting that went on forever. I could not just tear myself off it. I'm really sorry."

Hannah muttered, "That's okay, how did it go?"

"It went well," Adam said, "Just the same family talk, questioning the yet-to-be-married on when they were going to get married, to the married when they were going to have children, then basically reliving memories.

That was the part that seemed like there would be no end. Let me not bore you with mine. Do you want to tell me about your day?"

Hannah replied, "Nothing much. I decided to do some more writing for my book."

"Oh really, that's good," Adam interjected. "Hopefully, one of these days you'll get to tell me the actual story."

Hannah felt a smile form at the sides of her mouths as she thought, this man already sees himself in my life forever.

Adam interrupted her thoughts, "Sorry to cut you, please continue."

Hannah narrated all she had done in the day, from taking a break to check on her tomato plant in the garden, to the call she made with her sister. That was all, basically.

Adam jumped on the opportunity to ask about her family in detail. "I know you said you have six siblings. How many males and females are there?"

Hannah went on to explain, "We are four females and two males, all married except me. My brothers both live in the US. One of my sisters lives in Canada. The rest of us live here in the UK with mum and dad who live in Scotland."

"What about you?" she returned the question. It occurred to her that he had not spoken much about his family.

Chapter Sixteen

Adam knew Hannah had been honest with him and now it only made sense to tell her about his own family.

He began, "I am the third child in a family of four. My two elder brothers are married with children. They both live in Australia which makes it hard to see them often. My parents both live in the UK hence my regular visit here. It's also the reason I am planning to have a branch of our company here in the UK and move permanently here so I can be closer to them. My younger brother lives in the US while running a postgraduate course in the University of Michigan.

I have 3 nieces and 4 nephews who I love so much but I only get to see them twice a year except on Facetime.

We try to have family reunions once a year either in Australia or the UK. Ok, let me stop here," Adam chuckled "so I can have more to tell you when we meet face to face."

Hannah casually replied, "When do you think that would be considering the increase in deaths and number of infected persons?"

"Is it ok if I request that you send me a picture of yourself while I send mine?" Adam asked.

"I wouldn't know if you've checked my WhatsApp display picture before but my niece's picture is what I have there anyway,"

Adam added amidst a peal of quiet laughter. "Well, I'm not ashamed to say I've checked yours and I see you have the picture of a bible quote on it. I'll love to put a face to this new friend I've met."

"Ok, I'll send one now but it will be a picture I took before the lockdown. I don't think I've changed much anyway." Hannah replied.

They carried on their conversation till they began to discuss bible study. Adam talked excitedly about Faith and Hannah affirmed that it was one of her loved topics.

She narrated to him how her faith in God has helped her this far and how she has no other choice but to hold on to her faith in God as she was sure it would see her through.

Adam also shared how holding on to his faith in God had helped him, especially with regards to the contract he recently got signed.

Some of his friends and colleagues strongly thought no company would be willing to approve a contract in this season of an economic meltdown caused by the lockdown. "Despite it all, I held on to my faith that God could do even that which seemed impossible to men.

I also held on to God's promise in *Job 22:29*: *"When men are cast down, then you shall say, there is a lifting up; and he shall save the humble person."*

I constantly confessed the Word and it was amazing how God repaid my faith in him. I truly believe that if you trust God for everything, he will surely show up for you."

They continued till late into the evening until they were jolted by a phone call ring on Hannah's mobile phone. Though she wished she didn't have to end the conversation, she had to end the call.

The call was from her mother whom she has not heard from in a while, so she really needed to pick the call. Adam didn't want the chat to end either. He has grown into listening to her voice and it certainly made him happy.

Hannah had to speak with her mother anyway, so it had to be a good night.

"Good night, Hannah. It's been a beautiful time talking with you. I'll talk to you tomorrow," Adam wrapped it up.

"Hi mum!" Hannah said as she picked the call. "How are you? Sorry I haven't called in a few days. I've just been busy. How is dad?"

She replied, "We are both fine. We bless God. I was going to call you in the morning but I got busy. I just remembered now and don't want the day to pass without telling you the dream I had of you."

Hannah said, "Huh? Dream?? Mum, you and your dreams!" Her mum continued, "Yes, I had a dream of you this morning.

It seemed so surreal and I felt God repeatedly nudging me throughout the day to tell you."

She continued, "I dreamt we both travelled for a holiday, not sure of the country but it was a lovely sunny place. As we got there, we hailed a taxi to take us to the hotel. On our arrival at the hotel, we checked in and decided to go for dinner in their restaurant. We soon settled in our seats by the window.

It was a very pleasant ambience with mouth-watering delicacies. We had finished our meal and were heading back to our room when we met a man in the lift. He was tall, light-skinned with black curly hair, and commanded the aura of a responsible and respectful man.

He said hello to us but you didn't notice him as you were on the phone."

Hannah's mum continued, "We got out of the lift and I asked you if you thought he was good-looking. You said no as apparently, you didn't even see him. I was a tad unhappy as I felt he was your husband-to-be."

Hannah immediately interrupted, teasing her, "Mummyyyy, you most likely had that dream because of what you have going on in your mind."

Her mum cut her, "Let me finish. It's not what is in my mind but God telling me something is about to happen that will bring you joy. Anyways let me continue.

I told you in the dream that he seemed like a perfect husband for you and you smiled. The next morning, while going down for breakfast, the same man met us in the lobby and courteously greeted us, 'Good morning.'

Turns out he was there for a business seminar as he proceeded to invite us to the seminar. Your face lit up as he spoke about the seminar.

He urged us to come to hear him speak more at the seminar. I couldn't attend but you did after I forced you. You came home speaking so highly of him, and gushing over how much of an enlightening session the seminar was.

You were excited about the number of small business owners and influential persons you met.

The next morning we went for breakfast and he was the first person we met. You got chatting and exchanged phone numbers. We later got to find out that he lives in the UK as you and attends that Pentecostal church we visited the summer I and your dad came visiting in London.

I was about to ask him to join us for dinner later in the day when I woke up." Hannah's mother finally finished her narration.

Hannah listened the whole time smiling. She knew that the greatest thing her mother wanted for her right now was to get married so she wasn't exactly surprised at the content of the dream she just narrated to her.

There was one more thing though. Asides her mother's desires for her to find the right man, she also sensed that the dream was not just a figment of her imagination but actually a prophecy.

She thanked her mum for sharing, they did some quick catch-up chats, and she ended the call.

She settled for bed when she remembered her mum added that the hotel room number and floor level from the dream stayed stuck in her head.

She said she decided to read the Bible verse that dropped in her spirit, *Psalms 66:6 "He changed the sea to dry land, and his people went across the water on foot. So let's celebrate because of what he has done!"*

Coincidentally, the numbers in Psalm 66:6 rhymed with room number 66 and the 6th floor in the dream. Her mother had also encouraged her to read that passage of the bible, meditate and pray with it.

Hannah took her bible and decided to read the bible verse her mum gave her before going to bed and she got a level of illumination she had not got before.

She got the interpretation that this lockdown seemed like a red sea before her. She was initially clueless as to what to do with herself when the lockdown was announced. She worried so much over how she would cope with being alone but God gave her a friend.

Even though social interactions were limited, God has used this friend to ease the feeling of loneliness.

To her, this was a miracle. She was sure that just as God sent joy to her in the midst of the gloom of the pandemic, He was able to light up a dark situation

Chapter Seventeen

When Hannah woke up for her early prayer, she remembered that Adam asked her to send her a picture.

Contrary to what she told him that she would send an old picture, she decided to snap and send a picture of her current self.

On second thought, she didn't think she was looking too good just waking from sleep, so she decided to go with her initial plan. She scrolled through her gallery, found one she had taken three months ago, and sent it.

She said her morning prayers and went to the kitchen to fix herself some breakfast. While at it, her mum's dream flashed through her mind.

She said a short prayer and felt God tell her to prepare for a big surprise that would come her way. She whispered, "Thank you, God. I believe you."

She settled on her couch to eat her breakfast, after which she went into her garden to check on her plants. She was super excited at how her crop was growing. She could see some more tomato sprouting.

She couldn't hold herself back from taking some pictures of it. Just as she took the picture, she heard a notification alert on her phone. It was a WhatsApp notification.

Without taking note of the sender, she tapped on it and her jaw dropped instantly at what her eyes met. It was a picture that matched the exact description of the man her mother told her of in her dream.

For a few seconds, she was lost in thought. She found herself in her mother's dream. Whilst still in shock, another beep from her phone brought her back to reality.

The picture she was looking at was Adam. She smiled, Wow! God, you really have a big sense of humour and full of wonder! The Bible verse, *Psalms 77:14 "You are the God who does amazing things*

You showed the nations your great power" immediately came to mind. She was surprised as to how God could do this to her.

She was at an age and season when she really wanted to get marry but felt as though no one was asking her out and almost all her friends were married.

She had almost settled in her heart that God would make it happen in His own time; but for God to make to her meet Adam in a season of lockdown and in the most amazing way?! She was in awe and utmost gratitude to God.

Though she wasn't certain yet of Adam's thoughts towards her, she was truly convinced that this was a path ordained by God and regardless of the outcome, she knew it would be to God's glory and definitely a blessing for her. She quickly snapped out of her thoughts and remembered there was another notification that came in.

She checked it and saw it was a message from Adam. He thanked her for the picture and ask her to confirm she got his as well.

Her hands shaking as she read the message, she was hoping she wouldn't sound too excited when they get to talk later.

It had become a routine to call each other in the evening and talk about how their day had been, pray and have some period of bible study; and she loved it!

It took a lot for Adam not to shout or burst into singing when he saw Hannah's picture. She was exactly the type of woman he had always prayed for. She had a very beautiful face with that lovely spirit oozing from her.

There was this peace he could see in her face. Wondering why a lady this beautiful and peaceful yet still single amazed him.

He smiled, Maybe God kept her for me. He was so happy he felt like calling her immediately but when he looked at the time he realised it was too early.

This was the time Hannah had her morning prayer. He had to hold on some minutes more.

He sat down, looked at the picture again, thoroughly surprised at how God has led him on the journey of meeting Hannah. At the beginning of the year, he was so convinced that he was ready to settle down in marriage but because of his busy life, it had been hard.

He, however, kept hoping and trusting God to connect him with the right woman, and because of his faith, he knew God would make it happen.

What he never thought was that God could do it even in this period of limited social interactions. He knew that God would perfect the desires of his heart and bless him with what he asked for this year. His mind was filled with joy. He quietly prayed that Hannah would feel the same way.

In the beginning of the year, when he started praying to find the right choice for marriage, he thought it would be one of the ladies he had grown close to over the years in his church. Meeting new people has been hard and the only ladies he constantly met are the career-minded ones and from his interactions, settling down was clearly the last thing on their minds.

He also figured that his religious value was a sharp contrast to theirs so it was almost a dead end from the get-go.

For a long time, he thought Sister Dorcas would make a good partner for him but as much as he prayed about her, he never felt that sign that they were going to end up together. But with Hannah, it was just different. From the first day he spoke with her, he knew God had ordained their path.

After the pastor's call telling him of his dream, he had been praying to God to interpret the dream. Every time he prayed, the bible verse that always came was *1 John 5:14:* *"We can come to God with no doubts. This means that when we ask God for things (and those things agree with what God wants for us), God cares about what we say."*

He knew that God's plan for him was good and that God hears him and because he trusts in God, he was sure that everything would work for his good. God's words say in *Roman 8:28 "We know that in everything God works for the good of those who love him. These are the people God chose, because that was his plan."*

This made him confident that Hannah was the lovely pink flower he had been ignoring.

He was now ready to take it further with her.

He needed to figure out how to tell her and he hoped she would not find it offensive or attempt to stop their friendship

Chapter Eighteen

After the picture encounter, Hannah couldn't help but pray that God will speak to Adam and give him the boldness to ask her out. She believed that since the bible *says "he that finds a wife finds a good thing and obtain favour" Proverbs 18:22,* she had to pray for God to nudge Adam to speak to her. The thought of her asking him out was dead on arrival as far as she was concerned.

She briefly said a prayer to God about it when a bible verse came to mind, *Roman 8:28 "We know that in everything God works for the good of those who love him.* These are the people God chose, because that was his plan."

This gave her peace and an assurance that definitely God had a plan for her. Just as she finished her prayer, her phone rang. It was Adam.

"Hi," said Hannah in an almost blank tone. "How are you and how's work going?"

He responded, "I am fine and work is going well too. We've had some more good news with more contracts coming in and some of the small businesses we started are also thriving well.

It's a lot to be thankful for considering the current economic situation.

Did you hear in the news that the government is planning to ease the lockdown and allow people to go out but wearing masks and social distancing has to be strictly observed?

Our work-from-home policy will still be in place, however. I think that's the best decision for the company right now."

"Yeah, I heard the news too and I'm super excited I can finally go out!" Hannah chipped in. "I think the decision you've made for your company is the best one though.

The company will have to provide a new set up in line with Covid-19 standards as instructed by the government."

They went on and on about the pandemic, the lockdown, and the new normal.

In the midst of the conversation, Adam dropped the question, "What do you think about me and our friendship?"

Hannah was clearly thrown off guard by the question.

She didn't think Adam would drop the question that way. She couldn't even think of an answer.

"Why do you want to know?" she threw her question back at him but in a rather calm tone.

Now, Adam was the one somewhat taken aback by her response. For the short time he's known Hannah, he had established one thing about her: She doesn't hesitate to express her thoughts exactly the way it is.

Adam knew he had to say something so he mustered some courage and continued, "I just want to know what you think of me because lately, I have been thinking about you more than any lady I have ever met.

I have also been praying about it asking God for clarity on my feelings for you. God has definitely been speaking back to me but via bible verses which all seem like riddles, difficult to unravel.

I wish I could share some of the verses with you but that may have to be later. So in my trusting God, I'll like to know how or what you feel about me before taking any step."

"Please pardon me if I seem to be acting too fast. I just feel the need to get things right and on time at this phase of my life. Lately, I was praying, asking God for the next step and you showed up. I strongly believe that God must have a plan for making our paths cross hence instead of delaying any further, I felt the need to ask what you think about me too."

Hannah knew this was 'the time' she had been waiting for so she had to say something.

"I really don't know what to say but to be honest, I have grown to like our time together and I think I feel comfortable talking and sharing my daily activities with you. I sincerely look forward to our daily banter and I've grown to enjoy your company." Hannah said shyly but with every sense of certainty in her voice.

Adam felt relaxed and pleased that Hannah was honest with him. He had thought Hannah probably did not have as much feelings for him as he would have loved to but listening to her response gave him all the joy and assurance he needed. He thought to seize the opportunity to ask another thing from her and really hoped she would say yes.

With Adam's heart thudding loudly, he muttered, "Hannah, can I make a request?"

Hannah said, "Yes, you may."

Adam continued, "If you don't mind, can we have a video call? I'll remain thankful to God for using my obedience to join in the church program lockdown initiative.

I doubt we would have ever met due to our location and busy schedule. God definitely had a plan for making our paths cross. I remember the bible verse in *Job 22:29 When men are cast down, then thou shalt say, There is lifting up; and he shall save the humble person.*

Adam now felt he was babbling too much so he kept quiet and asked Hannah what she thought about the video call.

"I'm not a fan of video calls though but… it's not a bad idea to finally get to see your face so, that's fine, we can have it." Hannah responded.

"Thanks a lot, Hannah. We can have it tomorrow if that's okay by you."

Hannah agreed. After a few more minutes of Bible study, they both prayed and said their goodnight.

Chapter Nineteen

Adam could feel his heartbeat racing as he dropped the call. He thought how good God is to have answered the prayer he only began seriously praying beginning of the year.

It was funny how he had never felt ready to marry but barely few months after he began to feel ready, God was sending him his bone.

He was looking forward to their video call tomorrow. It was already nearly midnight but he didn't even feel sleepy.

He was too excited. All he could do was pray that she would not change her mind. Hannah stared at the phone for a long time thinking, Can this be God? Can this be happening?

Has God decided to give me my partner in this season when everything seemed dead and quiet? God had really made her find something positive from the pandemic. She closed her eyes and worshipped God.

This is a prayer she had prayed for so long and though she never ceased to believe that God would answer, a lot of people around her had questioned God in her life.

The icing on the cake was God using a period as the lockdown to show her His greatness and love. She was overwhelmed.

The hours seemed to pass by too quickly and soon it was morning. With excitement, Hannah woke up early with several Should I's and What if's running through her mind. Should I cancel? Am I really ready? What will

I say? Will I be able to sit still?

What should I wear? Should I wear some makeup? What about my hair? With all the chaos in her head, she managed to take a deep breath and decided to simply be herself. She put her hair in a ponytail and puts on some light makeup.

She decided to make the call on her patio because of the natural lightening usually present there.

Sitting in her patio surrounded by nature and her garden scenery usually made her feel super relaxed in some beautiful way. She quickly made her early morning coffee and attended to some emails before the call.

Adam could not keep to himself. He called his pastor to give him an update of recent happenings in his life.

The Pastor picked the call, "Hello brother Adam, how can I help you?"

Adam proceeded to narrate all that had happened even before the pastor shared the dream with him. He shared all the bible verses God had been giving him every step of the journey.

Adam also told him of sister Dorcas who he had met in church, took a liking to, prayed to God about her but didn't get any confirmation from God neither was there any deep connection.

However, from the first day he spoke with Hannah, he felt the connection and was planning to take it further with her. He wrapped his narration informing the pastor that he would need his advice and prayers.

The pastor had listened carefully without

making any comment. He finally said to Adam, "Can I ask you a few questions?"

"Please go ahead, pastor. That's why I called you," Adam responded.

"Ok," the pastor continued, "do you feel at peace when you talk with this lady? Do you feel she loves God like you will love your future wife to love God, and most importantly do you see her in your life as a help meet?"

Adam didn't even have to think about the answer. He said, "Pastor, the honest answer to all the questions you have asked me is yes. She exhibits all the qualities of the woman I have prayed for which made me know God ordained our path."

The pastor replied, "I will advise you to ask her to pray while you pray too.

I trust that God will place a common Bible verse in your hearts which will serve as the foundation blocks and light for your marriage.

God is a good Father and He will give you both that Word that will be an anchor to your marriage and through it, you will be sure of God's hands in it.

I am not implying that this is the only key to know if she's the one but this is what I prayed for when I met my wife and it was the best choice for me. Let me just pray with you." The pastor concluded.

After praying, he added, "God is laying a bible verse in my spirit, *Isaiah 52:8: "The city guards[a] are shouting. They are all rejoicing together. They can all see the Lord returning to Zion."*

I believe there will be rejoicing in this relationship. Please make sure you keep God as the foundation.

Let Him be the counsellor you go to anytime you feel confused and need help on the journey.

I know God loves you too much to make you fail. Make sure you court her with God's leading and His word."

Adam thanked him for his word of advice and dropped the call.

It was the time for their video call. Hannah was waiting expectantly. Her heart skipped a bit as her phone rang. She adjusted herself on her seat as she picked the call. Adam was even more handsome than the picture he sent.

He had a beard which was not in the picture as well.

The moment she picked and saw Adam, her spirit relaxed and she didn't feel the anxiety again. Meanwhile, Adam on the other hand was gobsmacked to see that the picture did not do Hannah any justice at all. She was more beautiful than Hannah in the picture she had sent.

"You are more beautiful than the picture you sent!" He blurted. "I should sue the photographer."

They both chuckled loudly.

They talked for so long, joking and laughing as if they had known each other for a long time. They talked about everything they could think of. Adam took the courage to tell her what the pastor said.

"Hannah, I will like you to do something for us both.

Right now, I am sure you know what my intention is towards you and I am praying and hoping you feel the same way. I would like to go into a love relationship with you. Are you willing to walk this road with me?"

Hannah could literally feel the butterflies in her tummy. She was bubbling inside but tried to hide it from Adam as she answered, "Yes, I will love to get on this journey with you."

Adam could not help himself as he screamed, "Thank you, God! I will like us to do something together. I spoke to my pastor and he suggested we pray together and seek God's face regarding this relationship before taking it forward.

He said we should pray for God to give us the same bible verse as a further confirmation from God as the One leading us.

It would also serve as our anchor scripture for our future journey."

Adam told Hannah to pray about it and write down the bible verse God gives to her. He said he will do the same. After talking for a long time, they both prayed and said goodnight.

During the call, Hannah found out Adam was a CEO and multi-billionaire owner of his company. He also owned quite a number of other businesses all over the world.

She felt relieved that she didn't know this about him before accepting to go into a relationship with him as this may have clouded her answer.

It probably could have gone the wrong way, she thought.

She may have turned it down as she wasn't usually drawn to CEOs because of their tendency to be arrogant as a result of their wealth.

She decided to pray and ask God to confirm if Adam was the right man for her. After a series of prayers, she fell asleep and dreamt of herself being promoted at work.

Her colleagues were gathered to celebrate with her and they brought a cake with Roman 8:28 written on it. She was about to ask them why they chose that inscription on the cake when her phone rang.

As she woke up, the bible verse continued to ring in her head. It was her sister calling, "Hey sis, how are you keeping?"

"I am fine," Hannah answered.

"Now that the lockdown is lifted when are you coming to visit or are you scared of leaving your home?" her sister teased her.

She laughed in return, "I have actually been

planning to call and give you some good gist."

"Really?!" her sister shouted. "Calling you today is perfect timing for this gist then. Why didn't you even call me since?"

Hannah laughed heartily at her sister's eagerness to hear the gist she had for her. "Just calm down and listen."

She told her sister everything about Adam, beginning from their last conversation about him to now and everything that had happened in between. It was a pretty long narration.

Her sister was so happy that she kept screaming excitedly.

Her sister asked if they could all meet up at their parents' place in two weeks' time. Hannah immediately agreed as she had been looking for an opportunity to step out of the house after a 6-month long break. She thought it might even be a good time to introduce Adam to her family.

They ended the call on that note, with Hannah telling her not to inform anyone in the family about Adam yet as she wanted to tell them herself.

Hannah had her shower and was about to prepare her breakfast when the bible verse came to her again.

As she got her bible to open to it, it occurred to her that she had seen the bible verse somewhere before.

Romans 8:28 "We know that in everything God works for the good of those who love him. These are the people God chose, because that was his plan." She took her breakfast to the patio alongside a pen and a notepad to write the bible verse down hoping it would be the same Adam has been given. She thought that would be the best news ever if the bible verses end up the same.

As she was about to eat, her phone rang. She was not expecting Adam to call this early and especially, not on a video call. She was very happy anyway so she quickly picked it.

Adam was too eager to find out about her bible verse.

He suggested they both showed their bible verse on the screen. Both unsure of what the other's verse would be, they displayed it and to their greatest joy, it was the same.

They were both thankful to God for showing up for them.

God had used what the world thought was a dark season to bring them into their season of light.

They continued their relationship over the

phone, had several virtual dates while building up their spiritual life together.

Few weeks down the line, the lockdown was finally lifted and they decided to have a proper date face to face. Adam booked a lovely and expensive restaurant for them to meet. As Hannah walked in, Adam's heart leaped for joy.

As Hannah saw Adam, she felt the cage of butterflies had been released in her tummy. She felt excited and anxious all at once. Adam could not take his eyes off Hannah. He felt she had an even more beautiful face than the one he had been seeing via Facetime.

They hugged each other knowing in their heart that theirs was a relationship designed by God and there was no turning back. They were now ready for this journey of a lifetime.

Chapter Twenty

The sky was blue with a few scattered clouds moving in simple, elegant strides through the sky. The water in its beautiful blue colour and gentle ripples as the wind connected with it made the water move in slow but steady waves.

Hannah walked elegantly toward Adam as he waved to beckon her. Hannah was curious as to why Adam decided they should have a date at the seaside; but without question, she went there. As she got closer, she noticed it was gorgeously decorated.

She had noticed this in all their dates. Adam always chose a beautiful venue. He had such good taste.

He liked things to be perfectly done, down to the bit.

The atmosphere was as peaceful as the sea with very few people at the beachside due to the guidelines still in place for people to observe the social distance.

"Hello, Adam. How are you?" Hannah said.

Adam hugged her as he said, "Hello darling."

Hannah looked around and the setting made her wonder what was going on, but she decided not to ask him.

"Come and sit down, darling," said Adam.

She said "Thank you," as she obeyed and sat down.

She was about to open her bag to present the little gift she brought for him. This had become a habit between them. They liked to exchange gifts every time they met. As she pulled her gift out, melodious tunes from a trumpet startled her.

Hannah looked at Adam as he smiled, with his face expressing his love for her. She felt relaxed as the trumpeter serenaded both of them while they sipped on their fruit wine.

After a while, Adam stood up, stretching his hands towards Hannah.

"Dance with me, Hannah."

Hannah laughed as she put her hand in his while she stood up.

Laughing, Hannah held on to Adam as they both twirled to the music.

It felt like they were alone in the world and wished they could be like this forever.

They were like that for so long that they

didn't know when the music stopped. They both continued to dance to the melodies of their heart.

The sound of a helicopter whirring above distracted them, and Adam pointed Hannah in the direction of the helicopter.

Hannah was astonished and tears dropped from her eyes as the helicopter let down a white banner with the inscription, "WILL YOU MARRY ME?" She turned to Adam, giddy with excitement, and met him on his knees.

She looked around again and could see her family, Adam's family, her friends, and Adam's friend now walking closer toward them.

Where had they been hiding all along? She couldn't believe it!

Adam said to her, "Hannah, the first time I spoke to you, I knew you were going to be a part of my life forever.

You were a confirmation to me that when you wait on the Lord, He shows up big. When the world was clothed in darkness, you were the light that walked as light with me. With you just a phone call away, I saw many doors opening up for me. You are my sunshine and today I ask, Would you do me the honour of being my wife?"

Hannah stood, thinking of how God had been good to her. At the point when she thought all hopes of meeting the right man were gone, God brought Adam.

Hannah with tears in her eyes, stretched her hand as she said, "I will."

Adam put the ring on Hannah's finger and

he raised her hand to announce to everyone standing. Hannah was still in shock as she saw their families and friends who had snuck up on her to celebrate this special moment with her.

The music played, and it was then Hannah noticed the mobile party hall was behind the picnic tent.

The thought of seeing and spending time with Adam made her oblivious to her surrounding; hence, she didn't notice the party hall as well.

They all moved toward the mobile party hall.

"Let the party begin," Adam whispered in her ear and he held her so tight as if she was going to change her mind and escape.

The night went on for so long. Hannah

could not stop touching her rings just to be sure it wasn't all a dream. At the beginning of the year, she never knew she would end this year with an amazing man like Adam to call her own.

No matter your circumstance, as long as you have God in it, you will sing a victorious song at the end.

Chapter Twenty-one

It was a beautiful Saturday morning. The sun was out shining; the sky was bright and beautiful, all arrayed in God's glory. It looked like they were singing some melodious songs to their Maker, while the world could only see the movement of its awesome beauty.

Hannah sat by the window admiring the awesomeness of God and giving God glory for making this day a reality for her.

In her precious space by the window, she could hear the exciting voices of her family who had gathered in this exquisite hotel just to celebrate her wedding day.

During their courtship days, Hannah and Adam had prayed for this day to come and for God to make it a successful one. Now sitting by the window, she was thankful that God had brought it to pass.

Hannah heard a knock and knew it was probably one of the professionals coming to get her ready. Her joy knew no bound.

"Who is it? Please come in," said Hannah.

As the door opened, Hannah's mum came in. "Good morning, my sweetheart," said Hannah's mum.

"Good morning, mum. Hope you slept well." Hannah replied.

"Your dad and I slept very well; like a baby. I am so grateful that God made me see this day.

I was beginning to think you and Adam would

not get married again after you delayed for so long."

"Mum, we just wanted to let the pandemic end so we can have everyone present. If not, we would have been restricted to a small number"

"Anyway," her mum interjected, "I am just glad the day is here."

"So, where are the professionals? Are they not here yet?" asked Hannah.

"I will check them. I will be right back. Do you want anything?" her mum asked her.

"No mum, I am fine. I guess I am too excited to be hungry."

Her mum smiled and asked, "Have you spoken to Adam this morning?"

"Yes, mum. He called earlier for us to pray together," replied Hannah.

Just as Hannah's mum was about to open the door, the professionals came in.

The make-up artist gasped as she saw Hannah's wedding dress. It was a gorgeous bespoke dress, sewn the exact way Hannah had wanted with the best material and expensive sequins.

The veil was a stylish, high-quality hand-woven lace and a lovely silver crystal tiara. Everything was perfectly made, with a touch of impeccable excellence.

The day was turning out just as Hannah had always envisaged it to be since her childhood days. It felt like the dream she had when she was a little girl was finally coming to reality.

Hannah was ready in no time and set to go to church. As she got to the entrance of the hotel, her family and friends were excitedly waiting to cheer her on.

She stole a glance at the ride that would take her to the church, and she was gobsmacked. Here was why. Adam had told her to not bother about a ride that would take her to church.

He had promised to surprise her. Seeing this right now, she was beyond surprised. It was the latest Bentley, with beautiful metallic gold colour, decorated with layers of lovely flowers and ribbons. She felt like a Princess marrying a Prince.

Once they arrived at church, her dad came down giving Hannah his hand.

The church was a picturesque sight to behold. Hannah was moved to tears, but she resisted the urge, as she didn't want to smear her pretty makeup.

Taking each step closer to the altar, her heart skipped a beat, looking straight into Adam's eyes. Though still far off for her to see his eyes properly, she could feel their hearts intertwined.

She could feel the string pulling her towards Adam as she feels like increasing the momentum of her step so she could get to the front quickly.

Adam could not stop the tears from falling the moment the church door opened, and he saw Hannah's hand in her dad's as they walked forward.

This is the day the Lord has made and we will rejoice and be glad in it Psalm 118:24. He wanted the ceremony to end quickly so he could have his wife to himself alone.

The ceremony, reception, and party were in grand style. Everything was beautifully organised, with many people in attendance. Everyone had a great time.

Adam and Hannah left for their honeymoon straight from the party, as they stepped into eternity and bliss together as husband and wife.

Printed in Poland
by Amazon Fulfillment
Poland Sp. z o.o., Wrocław